T0065162

DEACON

TEKOYA

authorHOUSE®

AuthorHouse™
1663 Liberty Drive
Bloomington, IN 47403
www.authorhouse.com
Phone: 833-262-8899

Published by AuthorHouse 07/17/2020

ISBN: 978-1-7283-6726-2 (sc)
ISBN: 978-1-7283-6725-5 (e)

Library of Congress Control Number: 2020912639

Print information available on the last page.

This book is printed on acid-free paper.

CHAPTER ONE

Cynthia was standing in front of her mirror trying to figure out what to wear. The last time she saw Mr. Carl he was on his way to prison for killing his step farther. It seemed as though people would never stop talking about it. She was fifteen then. The only thing that mattered to her at the time was her hair and her best friend Sissy.

Ten years later Deacon Carl now thirty-five is out and, he had sent her mother a letter asking if Cynthia could help him write his story. In the letter he explained that he had read in the paper that Cynthia wrote a book. He saw that it was doing very well. He hoped she wasn't too young to handle his story.

But at the same time he felt like she could do it without convicting him all over again. She was just a kid when he was arrested. When he wrote the letter he was surprised to see that Cynthia's family still lived in the neighborhood. He was happy it didn't come back unopened.

Cynthia was feeling a range of emotions before she went to meet Deacon. She even felt honored that someone thought her writing was good enough to help them write their life story. These last ten years had been an emotional roller coaster in her own life. After high school she had no doubt that she wanted to be a journalist and travel the world. After graduating from college nothing turned out like she thought it would. She started working for the local paper, writing stories on neighborhood gardening and, special events happening throughout the city.

This was definitely not what she wanted to be doing.

So in her spare time and during lunch breaks she would jot down some notes about how she was feeling and, which way her life was going. The next thing she knew she had filled up a whole note book. What she wrote helped her to realize she could not and, would not give up on her dreams. These precious words are what lead to her writing a book 'Educated Fool'.

Her grandmother always warned her not to end up like some people knowing everything but not having common sense.

"You got a good education now let it work for you," she'd say.

After three outfits she decided on some jeans and her pink top. She grabbed her tablet and, her phone and, the keys. She was half way down the stairs before she realized she still had on her flip flops. She slipped on some flats and, left. Deacon was only five blocks away but she decided to drive anyway.

When she pulled up in front of Deacon's house she fluffed out her hair. She put on a little red lip gloss and hopped out of the car. She looked up just in time to see Deacon push the curtain back in place and come to the door. She grabbed her tablet and, purse and went up the front steps. When Deacon opened the door he was wearing a pink apron. Cynthia smiled at that and Deacon looked down and snatched it off.

"Cynthia, how are you? You've grown into a nice looking young lady. So do you prefer Cynthia or, Miss Green?" Deacon said all in one breath.

"Cynthia is fine everybody still calls me that anyway," Cynthia said.

"In any case please come on in. Have a seat and you can put your stuff where ever it is best for you. I thought your mother was coming with you. I mean it's okay if you come alone. I just want you to feel comfortable," Deacon said.

"I'm fine being here alone besides my mom is volunteering at the Home today," Cynthia said.

"Can I get you anything to drink or, eat? I kind of got carried away with the breakfast. There's bacon and a few eggs left and, I'd be glad to make some fresh toast. The coffee is still hot," Deacon stated.

"That sounds good but please don't go to any trouble for me," Cynthia said.

"It's no trouble at all. Come on in the kitchen so we can get to know each other before we get started," Deacon insisted.

They talked about how Cynthia came to write her book. Cynthia thanked Deacon for breakfast. She said her grandmother always said food taste so much better when someone else is doing the cooking. Deacon was pleased that she enjoyed the food.

"May I ask why you chose me to write your story? I'm sure there are news reporters and all sorts of writers that would love to write it. I want to do it I just didn't feel I was experienced enough to write it," Cynthia said.

Deacon looked down at the table for a second then he answered her. He told her he wanted to start fresh. The reporters had their chance but, all they wanted to do was get rich. When they visited him in jail he assumed that they were trying to get the story before he died. I prayed that one day the truth would come out. Once it did, I was determined that they wouldn't make not one dime off my story.

Cynthia looked at Deacon for a few seconds. He stared back at her and then told her if she wanted anything else to eat she was welcome to it. Then they went into the living room and sat on the sofa.

"Would you feel comfortable if I asked you a few questions first?" Cynthia asked.

"Sure whatever works best for you," Deacon said.

"Do you remember how old you were when you and your mother first met Deacon Richards?" Cynthia asked.

"Yes I was about seven," Deacon replied.

"I read that your birth father had passed when you were very young."

"Yes my mother said I was three going on four. If it wasn't for my mother keeping those pictures of him I would not remember what he looked like."

"My mom showed me some pictures of your mother. They took some pictures together outside of the nursing home. Your mother was a very pretty lady. I understand she was a volunteer before she started working there. My mom said she would spoil the patients with her home- made cookies," Cynthia said.

"Momma was a beautiful lady inside and out.

You're right she made the best cookies on the block," Deacon declared.

Cynthia and Deacon smiled at that comment.

"My mom said she was real sorry to hear that your mother had passed. She really missed working with her,"

"Yeah me too," Deacon said.

"How did Miss Juanita and Deacon Richards meet?"

"She met that dog when she was working at the diner. I don't know if you're old enough to remember that little place that looked like one of those camping trailers. It was on Twenty-Fifth and Acorn Street. When I got out of school she would take me to work with her. Every evening he would come in to get coffee and pie. He always made a point of paying her a compliment and, buying me some ice cream. Of course I liked that part. But there was something about his smile that gave me the creeps," Deacon said.

"Finally he got up the nerve to ask her out. Six months after that he came in and popped the question.

All of momma's friends were happy for her. I was happy because she was happy. It was the first time I had ever been to a wedding. My mother looked like a movie star. She had her hair all done up in curls."

"She had on a white gown and I remember

that rhinestone belt that went around her waist and was tied into a bow in the back. It was also the first time I ever wore a tuxedo. I was so proud to walk her down the aisle," Deacon said.

"Did you have any more relatives in the city?" Cynthia asked.

"No after my daddy died that was it. My mom and dad were only children. So that's how I ended up staying with Miss Addie until momma got back from the honey moon."

"Oh wow I remember Miss Addie. She must have kept every child within ten blocks. She was the sweetest old lady and so was her banana cream pie. I wish the kids that live in the neighborhood now could have known her," Cynthia said.

"In any case after the honeymoon we moved

in here. I missed our old apartment. Plus we never got a chance to get all our things. Richards said he'd take care of it," Deacon said.

"The movers brought all our clothes and the boxes with our important papers. Good thing Momma had put our pictures in those boxes. A few of my toys and, momma's knickknacks and, dishes were in other boxes. Richards didn't think we needed anything else. So he told us the rest of our things were still in the house if we wanted them."

"How did your mom feel about that?" Cynthia asked.

"She didn't say anything until she found out the truth. She used the time we had left on the lease to go back and clean up. That's when we saw that the rest of the boxes were gone. She asked the landlord what happened to them and, he said Richards told him to throw them away. When we got back here, Momma confronted him about it."

"I have never seen her so angry. She asked him, Why did he tell them to throw away our things?"

She said he should have asked her first. He just stood there for a minute. Then the next thing I knew he just raised his hand and slapped Momma so hard she fell to the floor."

"Was your mother unconscious?" Cynthia asked.

"I wasn't sure she wasn't moving," Deacon replied.

"Oh my God, he did all that right in front of

you. You must have been scared to death. You were just a little boy."

"That didn't matter to him. He just kept standing over her yelling. He was saying she should never raise her voice at him. He wasn't going to tolerate his wife being disrespectful. I was so mad I kicked him and pushed him away from my Momma. I was shaking her and, calling her. Instead of him helping her he pulls me away. Then he is yelling at me saying he's going to teach me a lesson. He took off his belt and started beating me with it."

"Fortunately when he pulled me away I was holding on to momma's sleeve so hard I tore it. I think that might have woken her up. Once she was fully alert she tried to stop him. But he wouldn't stop hitting me. So she ran to the kitchen and got a knife. She stuck it right in his face. She threatened to kill him if he didn't let me go. He dropped the belt and me," Deacon said

"I never saw her look like that before. She told me to go get in the car. I could hear her telling him if this was the type of man he was and, how their marriage would be it was over. He was standing in the doorway looking crazy when we drove away," Deacon concluded.

"Wow, all that in one day," Cynthia exclaimed.

"Yeah, we went to a friend of my mother's. We wouldn't have come back but his pastor came by and talked with Momma a long time. He assured her that he wasn't taking sides. He wouldn't have come if he didn't think Richards wasn't sincere. He suggested they both come to counseling and that Richards go to an anger management program. Momma agreed to come back under those circumstances," Deacon confirmed.

"How were things when you all came back? Did he ever hit you again?" Cynthia asked.

"Things were okay for a while. Then Momma told us the so-called good news. The announcement of her pregnancy had him grinning like a jack-o-lantern and, I thought I would throw up," Deacon said.

"So I guess you were not really glad about having a brother or sister," Cynthia inquired.

"After a while I felt much better about it after I saw how happy Momma was. When Zoey was born I thought she was the cutest little baby in the world. I was very protective of her just like any big brother. Our lives were like something out of a fairy tale. Then she began to walk and talk. Then she became the original demon seed.

Momma would try to correct her and, he would pet her up. Then he would turn on Momma and say if she was stricter on me I'd be a better child. I could see that some days Momma was at her wits end. By the time Zoey went to school I hated her."

"To make bad matters worse Richards had become a holy roller. Every time the church doors were open we were there. I had to learn a new bible verse every night."

"If I forgot it I had to stand in the corner while they ate. Momma would never let me go to bed hungry."

"She always brought something to my room. What hurt the most was watching Momma slowly melt away. Giving excuses for his and demon seed's nasty behavior. I wanted so badly to see that knife wielding crazy lady again."

"Cynthia please forgive me, I hope I'm not keeping you too long. We need to talk about your fee next time. I don't know how this all works. I never published a book before," Deacon said.

"We have plenty of time to talk about fees. I'm just so happy I could help you with your book. If you want to stop now we can."

Before leaving Cynthia thanked Deacon for breakfast and having her over.

CHAPTER TWO

Judging the Book by the Cover

Cynthia could barely concentrate on driving all the way home. All she could think about was the things Deacon had told her. All she wanted to do was call Sissy and go somewhere and, unwind.

She thought about the hug he gave her before she left. It was strong but gentle. It didn't last long but, long enough for her to know he must have been working out. She remembered the pictures of him on the news and, in the news paper. None of them did him any justice.

That was the closest she had ever been to him. His hair was black and low cut. Deacon was really a nice looking man. He had deep brown eyes. He looked like he could see right through you but not in a creepy way. The shirt he was wearing wasn't see- through but she didn't see any fat. His voice was deep but not baritone. The kind you could listen to all day. She had to stomp on brakes at the stop sign. It brought her back to reality.

Cynthia ran into the house like a little child that wanted to show off a new toy. She called her friend Sissy. They planned to meet at the Oasis. Cynthia had told Sissy about the book so of course she couldn't wait to hear about Deacon.

Sissy asked about every crazy question that came to her mind. She wanted to know how he was looking at Cynthia when they talked.

Did he lick his lips a lot? How many tattoos did he have? How long was the nail on his pinky finger? Her final question was did he twitch a lot. She demonstrated that by jerking her head and blinking one eye. Cynthia could barely answer all her questions because she was practically on the floor laughing.

"You forgot something," Cynthia said.

"What?" Sissy replied.

"The doo rag," Cynthia said with a smile.

"Very funny," Sissy replied.

"Girl, I know you all hype about writing this story but, you need to watch your back.

"He has been in jail for ten years, Cynthee, ten," Sissy emphasized.

"He's not like G-man and them Deacon was the perfect gentleman, Cynthia said.

21

"Okay but maybe I should come with you next time. Do you remember how we used to walk on the other side of the street at Halloween to keep from passing that house?"

"Not counting everybody thinks Richards is still alive. People swear up and down they have seen him standing in the window," Sissy concluded.

"You don't have to worry about all that. Sure the house could stand a whole lot of upgrades. But I didn't see any ghost while I was there. I know my book did well but I feel like this is the biggest thing that ever happened to me," Cynthia said.

"I don't mean to burst your bubble. Everything sounds good. I just hope the book is not the only big thang that ever happens to you," Sissy said.

"Well right now I just need you to keep everything on the low. You and my mom are the only people in the neighborhood that know I'm writing this story."

"Well you know I got you. You might want to think about meeting him somewhere else. Eventually people are going to wonder what you are going over there for," Sissy said.

"You're right we'll come up with something. I just have such a good feeling about this story. So far it's been pretty sad. I've said too much already, Cynthia said.

"I'm happy for you girl. Maybe the next book can be about this best friend and her crazy side kick friend like me," Sissy emphasized.

Cynthia cocked her head one sided and looked at Sissy and shook her head.

"Alright it's time to go," Cynthia said. The girls paid their tab and left with their heads together while laughing out loud.

CHAPTER THREE

The Best Solution

Cynthia woke up to the buzzing bee sound of her phone. It was practically jumping off the table. It was her mother checking to see if she was up on time. She had never stopped doing that. Plus she had a few questions about Deacon. Cynthia told her as much as she could about Deacon. She said she would come over after work.

Cynthia's mom got a kick out of what Sissy said. She had to agree that maybe Cynthia shouldn't be going to Deacon's house alone. She suggested they think of a new meeting place. Cynthia admitted that made sense but, where?

Then her mom came up with the perfect

solution. She said Cynthia could use their cabin. She would not have thought of that since she had not been up there since her father died.

"Oh mom that would be perfect," Cynthia said with a smile.

"I do have one request if you don't mind. I'd feel better if Sissy or I go with you. We can find something to do so you can talk in private," her mother said.

"I'll ask Deacon but I think he'll be cool with that," Cynthia said.

She jumped up and gave her mother a hug. When she sat back down a question came to her mind.

"Mom what did Richards look like?" Cynthia asked.

"Oddly he wasn't a bad looking man.

Considering he always had a mean expression. I've heard women in the grocery store talking about how good he looked. One time when I went to wash clothes two ladies were having a real juicy conversation about him. I have even heard some things from the good sisters at church. They were all so fascinated because he had green eyes. Of course he was light skinned and had curly black hair."

"He was tall and had a big gap in his teeth he looked a little creepy to me. He looked like a human jack-o-lantern."

"Wow that's exactly what Deacon says," Cynthia said.

"Why do you ask?" Delia said.

"I saw a lot of pictures of Deacon and his

mother at the house but none of his sister or Richards."

"I don't blame him I don't think I'd want to see any reminders of them for quite a while. Have you read any of the old articles about what happened?"

"No, I don't want to spoil my creativity besides I'm getting the story straight from the horse's mouth," Cynthia said.

"I'm so proud of you and your dad would be too. I know this is what you wanted to do all along," her mom said with a smile.

"Well I better go home and get started. All I have so far are notes," Cynthia said.

"I want to complete a rough draft by the time I talk to Deacon again."

On the way home all Cynthia thought about

was how well things were going. Then she thought about Deacon's sister. She wondered if Deacon had his sister's permission to put her in the story. At this point she thought it was too soon to try and talk to Zoey herself. In any case she would ask him about that during the next meeting.

When she got home she called Deacon. He sounded like he just woke up. So she apologized for waking him.

He was glad to hear her voice. She told him all about the cabin.

"Cynthia that's the best thing I heard all day," Deacon said.

"Let me know when you want to do some more work on your story. I know I'll be available after work and on weekends. I also need to know how you feel about my mom and my best friend Sissy coming along some of those days." Cynthia said.

"I can't say I'd be comfortable telling my story in front of them. But whatever makes you comfortable," Deacon said.

"I understand and I know they will not interfere," Cynthia said.

They said their goodbyes and, Deacon fell back on his pillow. His mind went back to the dream he was having before Cynthia called. He closed his eyes and he could see Cynthia straddling him. Her body felt like silk as he ran his hands all over her breast and stomach. He rubbed his hands from her waist to her thighs.

He slowed his movements to match hers. He

was trying to make each moment last forever.

He felt the warm wetness flow from her body.

He was no longer in control. Afterwards he

didn't move he just held her in his arms.

CHAPTER FOUR

The Demon Seed

The next following weekend Cynthia asked Deacon was he ready to go to the cabin. She also told him her Mom and Sissy would be coming too. Deacon agreed to everything. Cynthia told him everyone would be riding with her. She said she would see him about nine a.m. Saturday morning.

With the exception of introductions it was pretty quiet in the car on the way to the cabin. Cynthia was really surprised Sissy wasn't saying a word. Delia Cynthia's mom cracked the ice by telling Deacon she was glad things worked out for him.

Cynthia was glad to make it up the hill and, around the road that lead to the cabin. She had forgotten how nice it was up there. They hadn't been up there for a long time. She forgot how much she loved the smell of the woods and, the light breeze off the lake. Even though Sissy was a city girl she enjoyed the times she spent with them. She and Cynthia used to pretend they were at Martha's Vineyard or even Jamaica.

Cynthia grabbed Deacon's hand and, invited him inside to see the cabin. Delia noticed it needed some dusting. She promised not to stir up a tornado.

"Cynthee, you might be more comfortable in the office," Delia said.

"That's a good idea Mom," Cynthia said.

Cynthia and Deacon went to her Dad's

office. It was a little dusty in there too. She got a cloth and wiped off the desk and tables. She asked Deacon to open the window. Just pulling the curtains open made the room look so bright.

"Did you want something to drink?" she asked Deacon.

"I could use a glass of water," Deacon said.

When Cynthia went to the kitchen her mom was checking the cabinets for food. Everything was out of date so she asked Sissy to go with her to the store.

She asked everybody how they felt about pizza. All agreed that was fine. Mrs. Carter promised she wouldn't be long.

On the way Sissy was a little concerned about leaving Cynthia with Deacon. Mrs. Carter expressed that she trusted Cynthia's judgment. Plus she didn't get any bad vibes from Deacon.

"Okay Miss D if you say so but, like I told Cynthee it's been ten years ten."

Back at the cabin Cynthia and, Deacon sat on the couch in the office. She asked him could they talk a little more about his child hood. He told her she could ask him anything she wanted.

"Did you have any friends?" Cynthia asked.

"Yes, Eddie and Beatrice were my best friends. We remained friends until the incident happened. I really miss my old friends. They practically saved my life. Since both their families belonged to our church I was allowed to play with them."

"Eddie and I were like brothers. We'd argue over video games and who was the best ball player. But we never stayed mad with each other long. Beatrice was like one of the boys in elementary school."

"Everything was going well until Momma had to go to a church meeting. Eddie's mom said we could come over there until Momma got back. Richards was still at work."

"This gave Eddie and me a chance to work on our school project. Beatrice was there also. We were almost done with it when Zoey came over to the table and said she wanted to go home."

"I told her to go sit down and that we had to wait until Momma got back. Beatrice offered to play with her."

"I don't want to play with her," she in a winy voice.

"I stopped gluing and told her to sit down, that Momma would be back soon. Of course she just stood there and rolled her eyes. Then she started to knock over some of the houses and trees we had glued in place."

"I grabbed her arm and told her I was going to tell Momma what she did. She began to yell and scream that she wanted to go home. She raised her hand to destroy the rest of our project and Eddie went to get his mom."

"Miss Justine told Zoey to come down stairs with her. Not long after that there was a knock on the door and Miss Justine told me to come down stairs."

"To my disappointment Richards got home before Momma did. Of course Zoey acted like a little angel as soon as she saw him. Then as soon as we got home she blurts out that I pushed her and I was acting grown."

"If eyes could kill I'd be dead the way he looked at me. I tried to tell him what happened but he didn't want to hear it. I told him he could even ask Miss Justine. He just yelled for me to get up stairs."

"I'm tired, I worked hard today. I know your sister is not lying," he yelled.

"He told Zoey to sit in his chair and watch T.V. until he got back. He came up stairs yelling I'd better be ready because he wasn't up for any foolishness. I know I hadn't done anything wrong so I refused to take my clothes off."

"You're going to learn to behave if I have to beat the black off you," he said.

Deacon and Cynthia jerked their heads

around when Sissy came in the office. Deacon went out to the car to help with the bags.

"Wow you two looked like you were having a pretty intense conversation," Sissy whispered.

"Talk to you later," Cynthia whispered back.

On the way to the car Deacon was thanking Mrs. Carter for letting Cynthia help him with his book.

"It was really up to her. I saw the lights in her eyes when I told her what you said. I feel like this book is going to be one of the best things that ever happened to both of you. I hope in the long run it helps someone," Delia said.

They brought the bags in. Delia washed her hands and got out the plates and cups. Cynthia went to wash her hands and when she returned Sissy was on one side of Deacon and Delia was on the other. So she sat beside her mother. They enjoyed the pizzas. Ice tea, bread sticks and, salad. On top of that Mrs. Carter brought a lemon cake.

While eating their cake Sissy turns to Deacon and says, "Excuse me Deacon Do you know my cousin Bank?"

"I mean I'm sure you ran into him in jail, everybody knows Bank. He didn't kill nobody or nothing he just robbed banks."

Before Deacon could answer Delia gave Sissy a sharp look. Cynthia just smiled nervously. Then Sissy apologized and stuffed more cake in her mouth.

"It's okay someone is always asking me did I see a sister, brother, cousin or baby daddy when

I was inside. I knew Bank a long time ago but I didn't see him inside."

"Oh, sorry," Sissy said.

"Everything was delicious Mrs. Carter," Deacon said.

"Thank you Deacon, Sissy and I are going to hit the trail to walk off some of this."

"I hope Cynthia will show you the trails before you finish the book."

"Come on Sissy we're not going too far. I don't know if they had a chance to clear off the trails," Mrs. Carter said.

"I'm okay with walking Miss D as long as we don't run into any large furry animals," Sissy said.

"Don't worry Sissy I'll protect you," Mrs. Carter said.

Cynthia and Deacon put away the rest of the food and went back to the office to finish talking.

"You were about to tell me what happened after Zoey told Richards that you were bad." Cynthia said.

"Well of course he didn't ask Miss Justine what happened. When he came up stairs and snatched off his belt. He kept trying to hit me and I was running from one corner of the room to the other."

"He screamed at me that I was just making things worse. Finally he grabbed me by the arm and I jerked away. I was trying to crawl under the bed and hold on to the leg of the bed.

"The only thing I could get was a shoe.

When he pulled me out from under the bed I threw it at him. It hit him in the face."

"In my whole ten years on the inside I never saw evil like the evil that came across his face. I thought he was going to kill me. Then he stumbled back against the wall and slid down on the floor. I didn't think I hit him that hard. Anyway before I could run to the door he grabbed me again and pulled me down. He was holding me down and trying to take my pants off at the same time."

"When he exposed my butt he began to beat me with that shoe. He had his leg and arm across me in a way so I couldn't move."

"Oh my God Deacon, that was awful," Cynthia said.

"Did any of this ever come up during your trail?"

"No they were so sure it was an open and shut case. I had a public defender. He thought that by revealing any of this it would make me look guiltier. I didn't know what to do."

"Did you ever tell your mother about the beating?"

"No, he told me to go to bed. He said I better not worry my mother. He said I was lucky he didn't take me over to Miss Justine's and beat me there. Of course I didn't want that to happen. I was still awake and crying when my mother got home."

"She didn't come up to check on me because he lied and said I wasn't feeling well and I went to sleep. When she asked about his face he said he had a freak accident at work."

"We could stop now if you want to. I'm sure you could use some fresh air," Cynthia said.

"Sure why not," Deacon said

"Come on I'll show you the trails," Cynthia said.

It was really pretty that time of year. Daffodils were peeping from under leaves. The squirrels were scurrying from tree to tree. The birds chirped as if to welcome them to the woods. Deacon said he had not smelled air that fresh in a long time.

They kept on walking Deacon was also amused to see a rabbit hopping through the woods.

"Now I remember why I love this place. It

has always made me feel at peace," Cynthia said.

"I can see why. I'm surprised we haven't run into your Mom and Sissy," Deacon said.

"I'm sure we'll see them soon, all the trails run into each other," Cynthia said.

They kept on walking until they ran into Mrs. Carter and Sissy sitting by the lake talking about old times. Mrs. Carter was recalling how Mr. Carter loved to play practical jokes. Not her or Cynthia had ever stayed overnight in the woods. So it wasn't a good idea to scare them half to death.

"Did you need more time Cynthee?" Mrs. Carter asked.

"Did you want to continue?" Cynthia asked Deacon.

"No I'm sure you have had enough," Deacon said.

"I want to thank you too Mrs. Carter for letting me come out here," Deacon said.

"I'm glad I could do it. We are really looking forward to this book being published," Delia said.

"Well I will admit I'd rather leave while there is still day light. That road can be a little tricky at night," Cynthia said.

Not much was said on the way back to the city. They all made comments about how nice it was to be at the cabin. Sissy told Cynthia that she was coming home with them.

So they dropped Deacon off first. Before he got out of the car he told Cynthia he'd let her do all the scheduling since he wasn't working right now.

Cynthia said that was fine with her. They all said their good-byes and waited for Deacon to go in the house. Cynthia could tell by the look on Sissy's face that she wanted to know what she and Deacon talked about.

"I already told you Sissy I can't betray Deacon's confidence. I know it's just us but one little slip and I know he'll never trust me again."

"I understand, I thought the look might help me get the scoop. Like I said I know how much this story means to you. I got you," Sissy said with a smile.

When they got to Mrs. Carter's house both girls went inside. Cynthia promised Sissy that they could go out for a drink but, she needed to talk to her mom first. They went to her mom's room while Sissy sat down stairs.

"Mom did anyone ever suspect that Deacon was abused?" Cynthia asked.

"Not really there were times that they came to church without him. We never saw him smile or try to make friends with the other kids. Little Eddie was the only child he'd talk to.

"When the men at church sponsored events for the boys Deacon never attended. Richards claimed he was a momma's boy. None of us questioned it. If he was abused that would explain why he kept to himself. Back then a lot of what people call abuse now was seen as discipline and, what went on in other people's home was their business," Delia stated.

"Well I understand people have the right to

raise their children like they want. It's just too bad that some children suffered because of it," Cynthia said.

Cynthia gave her mother a hug and said she would call her later.

CHAPTER FIVE

The Egg and the Testaments

Cynthia and Deacon decided to get together again that following weekend. When they talked on the phone Deacon asked her about her fee. She insisted that she was so happy to help him write the story she had not thought about a fee.

She didn't want to embarrass him by asking about money. She knew he wasn't working. He shared with her that during their conversation that his mom had an insurance policy. She made him the only beneficiary.

His lawyer helped him set something up so he could have money on the inside.

Not only that Deacon was due money from

the state since he was innocent. Then there was the fact that he never confessed to the murder. He knew that he wouldn't get that right away.

In any case before prison he had always worked.

So he expressed that he couldn't wait to be working again. When that was settled Cynthia told Deacon her mom and Sissy wouldn't be able to join.

Cynthia picked Deacon up early Saturday morning. They stopped by McDonalds to get sandwiches for breakfast. They decided to make some coffee at the cabin. Cynthia decided to let Deacon enjoy his coffee before asking questions. He got up and walked over to the window. She wanted to get started but they both seemed mesmerized by a robin pecking at the ground. Cynthia broke the silence when she asked him were there ever any witnesses to what happened to him.

"Sure people knew, and a few said something. I'm glad I have the opportunity tell the true story about what happened to me in that house. I used to sit in my cell and try to write it all down. Sometimes the memories were too much for me to bear," Deacon said.

"I couldn't tell anybody in there. I'd get so angry I punched holes in the walls and just end up in solitaire. A little voice kept saying I was crazy nobody cares about this shit. It's too late now it's over."

Deacon was still standing by the window. He raised his voice without realizing it. When he turned to face Cynthia her eyes were wide.

"Oh man, Cynthia I'm sorry I didn't mean to go off like that. I was just so angry on top of prison my Mom was dead. I hated my sister with a passion. I had night mares about him. I had permanent scars from belt buckles, shoes, and sticks."

"I'm fine Deacon you have a right to be angry. We could take a break now if you want to," Cynthia said.

"No I'm good," Deacon said.

"You asked if anyone knew if I was being mistreated. Yes, Mr. Harold one of Richard's friends. I don't know for the life of me how he had a cool friend like that. Mr. Harold was at the house. Zoey and I were upstairs. My job was to play with her to keep her quiet."

"Of course she had to go down stairs so she

could be seen. She ran into the kitchen. I tried to pull her back upstairs. She started yelling. Richards wanted to know what was going on. Zoey said I wouldn't let her get some water."

"The next thing I know she snatched the refrigerator door open. One egg dropped from the egg tray and broke. She ran straight to the living room and told Richards. He bust up in the kitchen yelling at me. I was so angry I yelled back at him. I tried to tell him that Zoey did it. The next thing I knew he grabbed me by the neck and slammed me up against the refrigerator. Mr. Harold came in to see what was going on."

"Jesus Richards, you gone kill the boy over an egg? He said.

"At that point Richards drops me to the floor.

He tried to play it off like he wasn't hurting me. I could tell by the way Mr. Harold was looking he knew better than that. Richards then tells me to clean up that mess before momma got home."

"The only other time I had some witnesses was when some people were at the house one night for bible study. Some of them were sitting on the couch and others in chairs facing them. Richards was in charge so he asked the couch people to recite the Old Testament books of the Bible. The chair people were supposed to say the New Testament books. They all sounded like a three year old just learning their numbers," Deacon said.

"Richards blurts out all yall going to Hell. My boy can say all of them. All of a sudden I'm his boy. So he calls me down stairs and tells me to say them. Momma was in the kitchen making cookies. I don't know what happened I couldn't remember the books in the right order. Each time I said it wrong he was getting angrier."

"He takes his belt off and threatens to beat me. Miss Ruth tells him to stop. She said none of them knew them why should I. He told me to pull my pants down because he was going to beat me for acting stupid. I stood there in front of all those people with my hands covering the front of me. I wanted to run out of the room. But all I could do was stand there and try to repeat the books in the right order."

"Every time I got it wrong he hit me. The guest finally started to get up and leave. One of the ladies said all that wasn't necessary. Richards insisted that I knew better. Finally

Momma came in to see what was wrong and dropped the whole plate of cookies."

"What the hell is wrong with you?" she yelled. Then Momma told me to pull my pants up and go up stairs. She was screaming so loud we heard everything."

"For some reason Zoey woke up and came to me. She wanted me to hold her. I heard Momma say she over looked how he treated me over and over again. She said that time he had gone too far. While she was yelling he must have raised his hand at her. She told him she wasn't a helpless boy. She said if he even thought about hitting her she would call the police."

"He comes out his face with a bunch of bull about he's trying to be the best father he can be. If he didn't try to keep me on the right track people would blame him if something went wrong."

"I heard momma say that patience and kindness was a part of being a good parent too. All of a sudden he turns the conversation around. He says she can leave but she was not taking his daughter. At that point he left. We heard the door slam and the car speed off."

"When momma came up stairs she held me and Zoey real tight. She was crying so hard I didn't say anything I just held her too. She said things were not going to be like this always."

Deacon noticed Cynthia was looking wide eyed again. He asked her if she was okay.

"Sure I just never knew that anyone could be so cruel to a child," Cynthia said.

She moved closer to Deacon and hugged him. He hugged her back.

"I'm almost afraid to tell you the whole story. It only gets worse," Deacon said.

"I know we are no way near the end of your story. I promise I will work with you to the end. Let's take a break I'd like to show you my favorite spot."

Cynthia took Deacon up a trail that led to a big, willow tree. The long thin limbs hung down around the trunk like a leafy umbrella. The tiny leaves stuck out and shimmered as the sun hit them. Cynthia grabbed a patch of leaves in both hands and pulled them apart.

"Welcome to my hideaway. Sissy and I used to hide under here from my mother. We thought it was so funny that she couldn't see us. Of course Sissy would always end up laughing out loud."

"We told each other our deepest darkest secrets under here. We practiced kissing to make sure we got it just right for our future husbands."

Deacon cocked his head one sided and looked at Cynthia. His deep brown eyes seemed to look right through her. Then he cracked a smile which made Cynthia laugh.

"You must think I'm pretty silly. I'm talking about trees and, playing hide – seek."

"No you are the best thing that has happened to me in a long time," Deacon said.

Cynthia was looking up at Deacon at that moment. He bent down and kissed her forehead. He started to apologize for the kiss. But Cynthia just looked at him in a way that said its okay. Then he thanked her for being a light at the end of the tunnel.

"That's a very nice thing to say. With everything that you've been through I'm surprised you can see a light at all," Cynthia said.

"I've waited ten years to tell my story. With your help I'm beginning to see it now. Can I ask you something?" Deacon said.

"Sure," Cynthia said.

"How come you haven't been snatched up already?

You're smart, beautiful and I'm sure you have a bright future ahead of you."

"I guess I'm just not ready. I want to see the world. I don't know I've dated a few people.

I knew for a fact they were not Mr. Right," Cynthia said.

"You deserve the best," Deacon said.

Cynthia made another opening pushing back the skinny limbs. They walked out and went back to the cabin.

"Cynthia if you don't mind I'd like to stop now," Deacon said.

"That's fine I'm a little tired too. Would you like to stop and get something to eat on the way home?"

"Only if I'm paying we can go where ever you like," Deacon said.

CHAPTER SIX

The Rolling Stones

Cynthia finally got an assignment that was exciting for a change. The paper sent her to the annual Unity Festival to interview the Temptations. That brought back memories of her parents dancing to their songs. She could not believe it she had written about everything from the knitting circles to the state's largest pumpkin.

She had her press pass and two free guest passes. She invited her mom to come with her. Then she was torn between Sissy and Deacon for the other pass. She had to admit she thought about Deacon first. Then she could just imagine the look on Sissy's face if she hadn't asked her.

To her surprise Sissy had a date and was fine with her asking Deacon. Cynthia tried to get her to spill the beans about the man. But Sissy wanted to surprise everybody at the festival. She called Deacon next. He was more than happy to go. Cynthia picked up her mom and Deacon. The festival was held at Rosemont Park. Cynthia didn't even have to worry about parking.

The smell of sausage, peppers and onions wafted through the air. The scent of cotton candy, popcorn, and elephant ears and fries made you want to eat all of them at once. The concert wasn't going to start until six. The interview was to be done after that.

As they walked along Mrs. Carter talked about old times. Cynthia loved hearing about coming to the festival when her dad was alive. Mrs. Carter noticed that Deacon was smiling and laughing along with them. She assumed he hadn't laughed like that in a long time.

"Deacon anything she says cannot be used against me. I was just a little person then. Momma would be at the pavilion checking out quilts and prize cakes and pies.

While daddy would spoil me with every sweet thing I was big enough to point to," Cynthia confessed.

"I can relate Momma would let my sister and I eat and ride until we dropped. The festival was among some of my favorite memories as a kid," Deacon said.

"You can say that again this festival is the one time people in the neighborhood could come together. It's been going on every since I was a child," Delia said.

They stopped along the way playing the games. Delia threw the balls trying to knock over the bottles. Cynthia cheered her on. Cynthia tried to spray the water into the clown's mouth. She was so close but no stuffed animal.

Then it was Deacon's turn all he had to do was make three baskets in a row. It was hard to do for some reason. After his next two tries he made it all six times. Cynthia picked a blue unicorn and Delia got the smiley face pillow.

"Did you play ball in school?" Cynthia asked.

"Yes I was pretty good but that's another part of the story," Deacon said.

"I don't know about you all but I'm hungry," Delia said.

Deacon and Cynthia agreed that they couldn't wait to taste one of those sausages. All three of them enjoyed more conversation and the food. They decided to walk off some of the food. Then they decided to go on a ride.

Cynthia screamed with each trip around the loop. The car they were in rose and fell and went backwards then forward real fast. At one point she held on to Deacon. Her mom made fun of her for screaming so loud. Cynthia had to admit she didn't expect for her stomach to flip like that.

It was finally time for the concert. They

headed for the tent. It was a good thing they got there early. The front row was filling up fast. A local singer came out first. They had to admit that he was really very good.

When the Temptations came out the crowd went crazy. Cynthia and her mom danced to 'Ain't to Proud to Beg' one of their favorite songs.

Even Deacon took Cynthia's hand and he swung her around when they sang 'My Girl' and a few more songs.

Cynthia was having such a good time she didn't see Sissy and her date walkup beside them. Sissy yelled over the music introducing her date. All of them danced until the last song was played.

Needless to say they all had a good time.

Cynthia did her interview and the Temps let her take some pictures. The festival was coming to a close and it seemed like it was a big success again.

They all hugged each other before leaving. Sissy even hugged Deacon. On the way home Deacon, Delia and Cynthia couldn't stop talking about the festival. Delia teased Deacon about his fancy dance moves.

He had to admit that he was surprised to see he still had it. It didn't take Cynthia long to get to his house. Deacon got out and thanked them again. On the way to her mother's Cynthia thanked her mother again for going with her. Then she finally headed home herself.

Deacon couldn't think of anything else that would make the evening complete except a nice hot shower. The water felt good as it ran over Deacon's back. He didn't think he'd ever get used to taking a shower alone.

Not counting being able to let the water run as long as he wanted to. He picked up the bar of soap it was sticky and soft. That caused it to make more suds. As he rubbed the soap on his body he imagined Cynthia was in the shower with him. He could feel her hands all over his body. She was standing right in front of him.

He could look into eyes and raise her hands to his lips and kiss them.

As soon as Cynthia got home she put her phone on the charger. She didn't want anything to happen to make her loose the interview. Then she remembered she left her pillow in the car. When she went to get it she saw Deacon's jacket. She brought them both in the house. She was glad to get out of her clothes and get into the shower.

The water felt so good Cynthia didn't want to get out of the shower. She wrapped the towel around her body real tight. Then she got another one and wrapped it around her hair. Back in her room she took the towel off and dried her feet. She went over to her dresser and got her moisturizer. Just then she did something that she rarely did. She looked at herself in the mirror.

The chill made her nipples stand out. She cupped her hands underneath her breast. She rubbed her hand over her stomach. She turned sideways and looked at herself from behind. She smiled and threw her head back like she was modeling. Cynthia sat on the side of her bed to put lotion on.

Putting lotion on the inside of her thighs made her think about sex. Cynthia tried not to think about it. She didn't want to do anything that might ruin her virginity. To hear her friends talk about orgasms was strange. She often wondered what an orgasm would feel like. She lay back on the bed and parted her legs. She let a drop of lotion fall on her love button. She felt the blood rush up to her face. She started rubbing it in a circle. Her buttocks began to tighten. She felt like she had to pee but this was way different. She was breathing heavy when it happened and she wanted to yell. Afterwards Cynthia pulled her comforter around herself and fell asleep instantly.

CHAPTER SEVEN

The Checkup

Deacon and Cynthia talked several evenings after the festival. They didn't work on the story right away. She wanted to take time for herself. She pampered herself each day. She got a manicure and a pedicure. She got a massage and went to the gym at the end of the week.

Apparently Deacon had the same idea. He didn't even ask Cynthia about the story. He spent some time at the gym and he looking for a job. He was disappointed that he couldn't get the job he wanted. But he got lucky when he stopped by the church.

He stopped to talk to his pastor about how

things had been going. He shared that he had faith that he would get a job soon. His pastor shared with him that they needed a sexton. Deacon accepted the job even though the pay was low. His pastor had been there for him so many times he was glad to help. Being at the church brought back some very pungent memories.

In a way this was where it all started and this was where it ended. He thought about the next chapter of the book. Maybe Cynthia could deal with it. He just didn't know if he could stand to relive it. Deacon decided to call her to see if she was ready to start on the next chapter. Cynthia let him know she was ready.

Deacon let her know that he would pick her up this time. He had received the first check from the state. All of a sudden things were getting better and better. He took part of that and opened an account. He bought a car with the other part. So he surprised Cynthia by saying he'd pick her up. Deacon also suggested that they go to a park he found while driving around.

She didn't mind working outdoors especially since the weather was going to be excellent. They agreed to go on that Sunday after church. They settled at a spot not too far from the main gate. The grassy area where they sat on a blanket was perfect. It was so green and well kept. The crepe myrtles that adorned the area here and there were in full bloom. Cynthia was thinking it wasn't the cabin but she loved being in the open. She wore her long sun dress with a bright orange and yellow and red print.

It tied around her neck causing her breast to sit up. She kicked her sandals off and pulled the dress over her knees and, feet. Deacon wore some jeans with a matching blue pull over polo shirt. The jeans fit him so well Cynthia couldn't help but check out his butt. He sat down across from her Indian style.

They chatted a little bit about how each other's week went. Deacon cleared his throat and cautioned Cynthia about the next chapter. She assured him it would be alright.

He started by telling her that, "Things seemed to be going well. I didn't have the slightest idea that he was setting me up for the worst night mare of my life."

"I was thirteen at the time. Demon seed was six. He had slacked up on the beatings every time I breathed the wrong way. Zoey even got a few smacks on her behind for a change. Momma wouldn't tolerate her lying."

"Richards started acting like he was interesting in me playing ball. He even put up a hoop at the back of the house. At dinner he would tell momma to give me an extra piece of meat.

"You can't expect this boy to play ball eating a few scraps. Eat up Deek you want to look good for the girls. Don't tell me you ain't got a girlfriend," he'd say.

"I didn't know how to take all of that attention. I didn't know what to say so I just smiled. Once or twice I even showed some teeth when he compared me to Michael Jordon."

"One Saturday Momma took Zoey with her

shopping. I stayed in bed a little longer. It was so good not to have Zoey banging on my door. After I couldn't sleep I went down stairs to get some cereal. I ate in the kitchen and drank some juice. Then I went to the front room and turned on the cartoons."

"I couldn't get used to the quiet. So I decided to shower and make my bed and get dressed. I thought maybe I could ask to go to Eddie's house. I got in the shower and just enjoyed every minute of it."

"I wrapped the towel around me and walked back to my room. Richards scared the hell out of me. He was sitting on my bed. I was scared to come all the way into the room."

"Come on in here boy. Why you acting like you seen a ghost? I just thought it was time for me to have a talk with you. When you start playing ball the girls get mighty fast. I want you to be ready for them."

"I heard the boys say that girls were all over them after the game. They never said anything to me so I thought maybe I'd better listen," Deacon said.

"I'm sorry Cynthia did you need to take a break? I just want to get through this part as quickly as possible."

"I'm pretty comfortable I'm recording as well as typing. But I guess I could stretch my legs," Cynthia said.

"Good, there are some food trucks around here. We can grab a sandwich and, drink, some ice cream whatever you want," Deacon said.

Cynthia put her iPod and her phone in her

carrying case. They found a burger truck and took their food over to the picnic area. More people had come to the park since they had been there.

They smiled at each other as they passed by children playing and couples lying on blankets kissing. They decided to stay under the shed for shade.

"Do you want to stay under this shed?" Deacon asked.

"I really don't want to move. If a family comes then we will go. Besides I'm really enjoying this shade," Cynthia said.

"If you prefer to go to the cabin I understand," Deacon said.

"No, I like this park I wouldn't mind coming

back here one day. We can start when were done eating," Cynthia said.

"That just hit the spot, now where was I?" Deacon asked.

"Sure did, do you want to continue?" Cynthia asked.

"Yes, we can," Deacon said.

"You had just come out the shower and, Richards was in your room," Cynthia said.

He said," Come on over here and sit down. I need to show you something .I should have done this before now. You don't have to be scared."

"I was scared anyway I didn't know what the hell he was talking about. But I soon found out," Deacon said.

"I talked with your mother and she said it was okay for me to help you. She said that she thought you might feel better if I did it instead of a strange doctor. He said he would let her know how I was doing. I could barely look him in the eye. I felt weird," Deacon said.

"He told me to stand in front of him and take off the towel. He said if I was cold I could put it around my shoulders. He pulled me up to him I didn't want to look in his face. I just kept looking at his hands. Those same hands that had slapped me and, held belts and shoes to hit me with."

"He started to rub and pull on my penis. I stepped back a little but he told me to hold on he was almost done. He continued to rub and pull until I had an erection."

"I didn't know what to do. I felt sick to my stomach. Then he let me go and hugged me and said it was normal. He said the checkup went just fine."

"He told me to go use the bathroom. He said that should help bring it down. He was watching me while I was peeing. I don't know for sure but, I think he was jerking off. He had his hand in his pants."

"Oh my God Deacon that's what these people do to molest kids. I can almost understand how you felt. I feel sick just hearing about it. To use your mother to do it that was the lowest. I've read different articles but this is a first. I'm so sorry. I know you didn't kill him but you certainly had a reason to," Cynthia confirmed.

"We can stop now if you like," Deacon said.

"No, I'm fine at some point did you ever tell your mother?"

"No that's just it because he was saying that my mother wanted him to do it. Then to add that bull shit about ladies don't like doing those things especially mothers. Well I thought it was alright. Even though I was uncomfortable, I didn't know who or what to tell someone."

"I never heard Eddie say his dad did that to him. And I certainly was not going to ask him about it," Deacon added.

At this point they were the only ones under the shed. So Deacon didn't hold back from telling the rest of the story.

"So what happened after that day?" Cynthia asked.

"He said he'd let me know when I was due for the next checkup. A few weeks later Momma took Zoey with her to a church meeting. This time we were sitting in the front room watching T.V. About an hour after they left he started talking to me about how I was feeling."

"I told him I felt fine. He said that my momma was so happy to hear that the checkup went just fine. He lied and said that was why she baked a cake that night."

I smiled at the thought of doing something that pleased my mother. Then he said it was time for my next checkup

"He told me to take my pants off and underwear. He told me to bend over and, do a toe touch. When I did he fondled by me. He said they felt fine and to continue doing toe touches. He said not to turn around. I heard his zipper go down and I stopped."

Deacon took a long pause and a deep breath.

Cynthia told him it was okay he didn't have to say anymore. He told her he just needed a minute.

"I just hated myself for being so stupid. The next thing I knew he took off his pants and draws. Then he stood beside me. He started doing toe touches too. He said something about grow ups needed checkups too. That's why he needed me to check him. He said he trusted me to do it."

"He took my hand and placed them on his balls. He wanted me to rub them. He was holding my hand very tight while he rubbed his self with it. He was pulling me close to him.

I turned my head sideways to keep from looking at him. Then the phone rang. My mother said she was right around the corner and was apologizing for taking so long. Something in me wanted to shout for help.

"We put our shorts and pants back on and he said something about momma would be so proud of me. That's the most I can do. I can't talk about it anymore. Hope I didn't gross you out too much," Deacon said.

"It wasn't your fault," Cynthia assured him.

They walked back to the car. The two of them didn't say anything on the way home. Every now and then she would look over at him. He just stared at the road. When he stopped in front of her house she hugged Deacon for a long time before she got out of the car.

CHAPTER EIGHT

Blood Is Thicker Than Water

Deacon called Cynthia on and, off for a few weeks to see how she was doing. She continued to assure him that she was fine. They decided to meet at the cabin the following Saturday. Deacon asked her did she want to bring her Mom or Sissy. She said that she felt like it was better if they didn't have any distractions.

Deacon arrived at the cabin about ten minutes after Cynthia. That gave her plenty of time to get the coffee started.

She made a few turkey sandwiches and, got out the fruit and chips.

"You didn't have to do this," Deacon said.

"I know but I was hungry," Cynthia said.

They talked about how each other's week was going. They talked about their jobs. Then they decided to take their coffee to the den.

Cynthia was a little hesitant to start. She feared the worst was yet to be revealed. But she asked Deacon was he ready to start anyway. He said he was ready.

"After the last incident Momma didn't have any more meeting for a month. Richards started to act like his old self. He was yelling at me for little or no reason. Then it got to the point he was yelling at everybody."

"One Saturday Momma let him know that she and Miss Justine were going shopping. She said she was taking Zoey with her. I asked could

I go over to play with Eddie but Miss Justine said he was at his grandma's."

"Richards was in the back yard working on the lawn mower. He told my momma that we were going to cut the grass and clean the yard. He tried to work me do death. But I kept up with the pace anything was better than getting a beating."

"When we were finally finished he told me to go inside and shower because I smelled like a skunk. I couldn't argue with that so I did. When I came out the shower there he was again."

"Come on boy I ain't got all day. Let me see how you been doing. He started rubbing and pulling on my penis. He asked me did I have any pain down there. I told him no. He said it looked like I was doing fine and left out of the room."

"Then he went to their bathroom and took a shower. I had just put my pants on when he came back in my room wearing his robe. I felt like running and screaming. There was something about that jack-o-lantern smile that gave me feel sick."

"I thought I had done something wrong. He said that he had to do one more thing. He said this time it would hurt but he would take it easy.

"He asked me was I ready for it? I shook my head slowly yes."

"I'm glad your momma took little Zoey with her today she would have just gotten in the way," he said.

"When men are trying to check each other

you don't need a noisy little girl around. He was making me nervous. I never heard him say anything bad about Zoey."

"He told me it was the last thing we had to do. He said again I had done well so far. He even said he was sorry that I had to take my pants off again. He told me to stand close to the side of the bed. He told me to bend over. I still had my shorts on so he pulled them down."

"I started to shake, he told me not to be scared. He said he didn't want to hurt me but it had to be done. I had my head turned sideways on the bed. He had his hand on my back and put his finger inside me," he said.

"I cried out for him to stop. He wouldn't he just kept saying it was better to get it over with now. He was rubbing my back and saying its okay while he continued to ram his finger inside me."

"I told him I felt like I was going to throw up. He said that I was supposed to feel that way. I wouldn't be a man if I didn't. He let me go to the bathroom. It seemed like everything in me came out. After that he told me to bring him the Vaseline off my dresser. He told me to bend over again so he could put some on me."

"That was supposed to stop it from hurting. At that point he was raping me and all I felt was pain. I cried out for him to stop but he wouldn't."

"What he didn't know was that my mother had come back home. She let Zoey go home with Miss Justine. She was still getting stuff out of the car. When she did hear me she ran up stairs he was so busy raping me he didn't hear her come in."

"She screamed something when she opened the door. Then she ran back down stairs. He pulled out and stumbled into his shorts. Then he ran after her. I fell to the floor I couldn't stop crying.

"I could hear Mamma calling him every name in the book and threatening to kill him. He was telling her to put the gun down. He was saying that he was sick and needed help."

"The next thing I heard was him screaming."

"This bitch just shot me.

"I thought Momma was going to kill him. I was scared out of my mind. I put my shorts on and ran down stairs I begged momma to stop. She looked like a crazy person. She had only nicked him in the arm. I remember crying and telling my mother I was sorry. It was my fault he was only trying to check me so you won't have to take me to the doctor. She was crying and shaking still pointing the gun at him."

"I was standing there holding my arms out. He is behind me by the door and momma is in front of me. She is looking from me to him, me to him."

"Doctor what are you talking about Deacon?" she asked.

"He said you wanted him to check me because ladies don't like doing that stuff. Did I do something wrong? Ma it's my fault please don't be mad," I pleaded.

"No, no, no, baby you didn't do anything wrong. Deacon, go upstairs baby you're bleeding. I'm not mad at you haven't done anything wrong," she said.

"The whole time she was looking dead at him. When she lowered the gun I turned to go up stairs. Before I could take the first step Richards grabbed the car keys off the nail by the door and ran out. Momma shot at him again. The bullet hit the door but missed him. After that she came up stairs and just held me and cried. We both cried for a while. My heart ached to see momma in so much pain. She told me that she was so sorry for what happened to me. She said it would never happen again. After she washed my face she asked me to tell her everything."

"She reported him to the police. I had to go to the doctor and give a statement. He was arrested but I'll talk about that another time."

"You want to hear something funny. Before all that happened I finally got up the courage to ask Eddie did his daddy ever check him. I never explained what I meant. He said his mom and dad did but, the account got overdrawn and they couldn't do it anymore."

Cynthia's eyes grew wide and all of a sudden she just started cry.

Deacon was turned around to the window so he couldn't see how pale she was. When he turned around he went and put his arm around her. Cynthia's face was buried in her hands. Deacon began to apologize for everything.

"It was not your fault. None of it was your fault," she said through her tears.

Deacon held her until she stopped shaking and crying.

CHAPTER NINE

Friends

Deacon didn't call Cynthia for a week. His emotions were all over the place. On top of that the night mares had started again. He remembered how he used to wake up in the middle of the night screaming for Richards to stop.

His mother spent a lot of sleepless nights staying up with him. He felt guilty that she was never the same again. It was months before he saw her smile.

He didn't have to face Richards at a jury trial. Since Richards admitted to what he did. As usual he talked his way out of going to jail.

He got five years probation and had to go to therapy. He wasn't allowed to be anywhere near him or Zoey. There were times Deacon wished they could have gone to court. To know that Richards got to walk around free made him angry. When he wasn't having night mares he was dreaming about different ways to kill Richards.

The only saving grace was that nobody in the neighborhood knew exactly what happened. His mother talked to Miss Justine and Miss Addie about it. They were her closest friends she knew they would never tell anyone. Deacon knew that never in a million years could he tell Eddie or Beatrice.

Deacon was going crazy trying to figure out what would be a good time to call Cynthia.

He was afraid that she would not want to hear anymore. He decided to talk to his pastor. His Pastor suggested that since Cynthia had stuck with him up to this point it showed that she was a very mature and strong young lady.

He told Deacon to call her and see how she's doing first. Maybe they should get together just for coffee or dinner. Then give her time to call him to finish the book. His pastor thanked him for sharing his story. He said that Deacon would be able to help a lot of young men with his story one day.

Deacon was surprised that Cynthia was so glad to hear from him. It turned out that she had some kind of virus and she was wiped out for a week.

That was the only reason why she had not

called. She agreed that it was time for her to get some air.

She met Deacon at Soul to Soul restaurant. They spent most of the time talking about the meal. Cynthia was just glad to be able to eat again. They talked about summer coming up and Sissy and her mom. He was happy to let her talk for a change. Then there was her smile he could see her smile like that all day.

Somehow the subject got on marriage. Cynthia said she loved the idea of the gown and tux and all that. She made him laugh when she said that if she didn't let Sissy be her maid of honor she'd have to kill her. She said she would also look forward to that day because she would love to see her mother dressed up for a change.

"My mother is a beautiful lady. It's so hard

to get her to do something for herself. I really want a wedding for her more than myself. They are so expensive. If it was left up to me I'd just go to a justice of the peace and have a big old reception. We'd drink champagne and dance the night away," Cynthia said.

"Afterwards my hubby would sweep me up and we would go to some exotic island."

Cynthia's eyes just sparkled the whole time she was talking. Deacon loved every minute of it. He didn't know who she was thinking of but the whole time she was talking but, he imagined that he was the groom.

"I must sound like I'm ten years old I included everything but a prince and, a pumpkin carriage," Cynthia said.

"Not at all after our last meeting it's good to

see your face light up. A young lady as beautiful as you should have the wedding of her dreams. I'm still wondering what you're waiting for and why."

"Well I didn't tell you everything about myself. At this point there is no reason for me to keep secrets from you. I'm a virgin, Deacon."

Deacon didn't say anything for a minute. She explained that some of the guys she went out with just automatically thought she was ready to go. When she told them she wasn't they didn't call anymore.

"In a way I was kind of glad I didn't have to feel pressured into doing anything I wasn't ready to do," Cynthia said.

"I could understand that and you shouldn't," Deacon said.

"What about you? I can't believe there wasn't a special lady in your life. You are very handsome and you're in great shape. Sorry didn't mean to go too far," Cynthia said with a smile.

"Well I don't have to tell you my head was all messed up. I felt like a freak. But I didn't ask you out to talk about that. Let's just say I tried but like you I wasn't ready. I know it sounds weird for a grown man to say."

"When my day came it was awkward and it cost me a dear friend. Again we are not going to talk about the tragic life of Deacon Carl," he stated.

"Hey how about some Sweet Frog?" Deacon asked.

"You don't have to ask me twice," Cynthia said.

They had ice cream and even went to a movie. On the way home Deacon asked Cynthia if she felt like riding. She agreed with him that she didn't feel like going home right then. Cynthia shared stories with Deacon about the fun family used to have on road trips.

It was a relief for both of them to just be together and not talk about anything bad. Cynthia was so relaxed she went to sleep on the way but home. Deacon could barely keep his eyes on the road. He was so busy looking at Cynthia.

Delia called Cynthia one Saturday morning to see if she and Deacon were going to the cabin. It just occurred to Cynthia that it had been a few weeks since they worked on the book. She wondered why her mom had asked. She said she was going up there to do some fishing. She knew they were still working on the book and she felt better just knowing she wouldn't be there by herself.

When Deacon got the call he said he'd be glad to go but he'd have to come a little later. He said the church was having a special function and he was going to help set things up. Cynthia said she would ride with her mom.

She said she would look forward to seeing him later.

Cynthia didn't talk much on the way and Delia didn't inquire as to what was wrong.

Before they got to the cabin Delia stopped to get food. This time she bought chicken, a veggie tray and extra ranch dressing. They decided to get cranberry juice and ginger ale.

"Mom I don't see why you aren't big as a house," Cynthia said.

"I guess I never will get used to only cooking for myself. I can't remember a time when we came up here and didn't eat. How's the book coming?" Delia said out a clear blue.

"I wondered what was taking you so long to ask," Cynthia said with a smile.

"It's fine, a little rough but fine. It's amazing the things some people go through in life and survive.

"That's true, is Deacon coming?"

"Yes, he said he had to help set up the tables at church. Did I tell you he has a job as their sexton?"

"That's great I heard something on the news about him getting some of that money the state owed him," Delia said.

To their surprise Deacon arrived to the cabin only a few minutes after them. Cynthia went out to greet him. She said she hoped he had not eaten because her Mom just brought out the store. Deacon just smiled he told her had not.

.

They went inside and Delia was already enjoying lunch. She said she didn't want to have to stop to eat once the fish started biting. Cynthia and Deacon washed their hands and joined in. Deacon Thanked Delia for bringing his favorite chicken wings.

Hall/Deacon/pg.82

"It feels good to see a man enjoy a meal.

When the time permits you are welcome to come by and get a good home cooked meal," Delia said.

"I'm definitely going to hold you to it," Deacon said.

"Well I'd better get started the temperature is supposed to go up at noon. You eat all you want."

After her mom left Cynthia asked Deacon did he want to work on the porch or in the den again. He said the porch and they brought their drinks out there too.

As usual Cynthia didn't hesitate to start. She told Deacon that they left off with him talking about his first love.

"I wish it had been like that. What happened was I had just graduated from high school. I was disappointed because I was looking forward to a basketball scholarship but just my luck during our last game of the season a player from the other team fell on my foot somehow."

"I tried to get up but my ankle was all messed up one of the bones were broken. It took weeks to heal. Every time I went up for a shot and came back down the pain was unbelievable. Well no more scholarship. Momma tried to encourage me to at least go to a community college and study engineering. She knew I liked tinkering with things."

"I didn't want to disappoint her so I went. I really enjoyed learning about that stuff. I was good at math and I was leaning towards building something that might improve the environment. One night I was on my way home and I saw a car in front of the house. I had never seen it before so I just thought it was the landlord."

"I went in the house and I heard Momma and a man talking. As soon as I heard Zoey say daddy don't leave. I flew into a rage and ran into the kitchen. I didn't say a word I just grabbed him by his coat and started punching him in the face. I didn't stop I knocked him down I began kicking him."

"Momma and Zoey was screaming for me to stop. He went limp and, I thought he was dead."

"Zoey came over to him crying. I looked at my mother and asked her why? She said she didn't know he was coming. He staggered up and left slamming the door. Later she did say that he was talking about going to court to see if he could have visits with Zoey."

"He had some nerve. There's no way I would trust him with my child," Cynthia said.

"He got visitation but momma and worker had to be present. At that point I knew I couldn't stand being in the house while he was there I wanted to kill him. It was all I could do to keep from going down stairs and doing just that. I told my mom I was going to stay with Eddie and Beatrice."

"It took months but my mom finally got divorced. I had been helping mom with the bills. I told her I would continue to help her. Of course she was more concerned about me going to school.

"Eddie and Beatrice were happy to have me. On top of that the rent was very reasonable. So it was not hard for me to keep things going."

"I never really told Eddie and Beatrice the truth about why I beat up Richards. I just let them think what they wanted. I was glad to have somewhere to go. Eddie even got me a new job at the warehouse where they worked. Beatrice and I had the day shift. Another good thing was that we were just across town so mom didn't have far to come."

"Did you ever think that he would harm Zoey?" Cynthia asked.

"No when my mother and the worker never let her out of their sight."

"Deacon if you don't mind I want to take a break," Cynthia said.

"Sure I could stand to stretch my legs too. And if there is any left I'd like a few more of those wings," Deacon said.

They went inside the cabin to get more to drink and a snack or two. In the middle of a bite Deacon remembered that Delia was still out by the lake.

Cynthia had completely forgotten her mother had been fishing all that time. So they decided to go down the trail to check on her.

Delia almost forgot they were there too the fish were biting and, she was having a great time. She told Deacon he was invited to a fish dinner that night. The only catch was he had to help clean them.

Deacon let her know he'd be delighted to clean them. Cynthia told him he was in for a treat that her mother made the best coleslaw in the neighborhood. That was their favorite thing to have with fish and, corn on the cob.

"I have to admit I love all this good food. Momma was the same way she couldn't stand the thought of anyone or anything going hungry," Deacon said.

Cynthia told her mother they were going back to the cabin. Once they got back they decided to finish talking in the den. Deacon told Cynthia that Beatrice was always trying to fix him up with one of her friends.

"I remember this one girl was all over me. All of us had just got back from the movies. Eddie and Beatrice went in their room and the girl and I sat on the couch. The next thing I knew she was straddling me and grinding hard as she could."

"Instead of her turning me on, she just made me feel sick. She was perfect from head to toe. I don't know what happened. It was the first time I'd been out with anyone. Maybe she just moved on me too fast."

"Anyway she got mad because I didn't respond to her and slammed the door on the way out. I went after her and offered to take her home. She yelled at me to get away from her. She said nobody has ever rejected her like I did. We were walking while she talked. Before we knew it I'd walked her to the bus stop. I watched her get on before walking away."

"The next night after Eddie went to work Beatrice confronted me because her friend told her she thought I was gay. I told Beatrice that I was just trying to be a nice. I didn't believe in jumping on a girl like some animal."

"I wouldn't share this next chapter with you

but it is a very important part of the story," Deacon said.

"There is no need for you to hold back. I know you are not trying to shock me. If this is what happened then that's what happened," Cynthia said casually.

"Beatrice tells me that the girl would have loved for me to act like an animal. She said that was why she hooked us up. Then Beatrice walks up to me real close and asked me if I was gay."

"She said she wouldn't tell Eddie. I told her that I wasn't gay. I was about to tell her what happened and she cut me off. She went into a speech about how in all the years she and Eddie knew me they never saw me with a girl."

"The next things I knew Beatrice takes my hand and put it inside her robe and drags it up between her legs. I stood there like a deer in head lights. I didn't pull away. She moved my hand in a circle until my fingers were wet.

"She lifted my hand up to her lips and licked my fingers. When she stopped she stood back and just stared at me. I couldn't move. I knew going this far with my best friend's girl was dead wrong."

"I hope what I'm about to say doesn't sound too judge mental, but I really didn't expect the story to go in this direction," Cynthia said.

"Neither did I, I knew eventually I'd lose the only friend I ever had. The more I tried to resist her the more I wanted to be with her. Beatrice was the only girl I had ever known or trusted. She told me that she didn't know what was holding me back but she was willing to take things slow. She tried to justify what was happening by saying we were all friends and friends help each other through hard times."

"She would scratch head and grease my scalp. We'd give each other massage. I'd paint her toe nails. We did all the things that couples do except go out. One morning Eddie was running late and went out the door without locking it. Neither of us thought to check it."

"Beatrice and I were making love and she was so loud we didn't hear her friend Melanie."

"She didn't call out she just bust open the door. She gasped and turned and ran out of the house. We assumed she was going to tell Eddie the same day. Instead she wanted me to make love to her so she wouldn't tell. It was bad enough that I had betrayed Eddie but now I'd be betraying Beatrice too."

"I refused to do it and of course the shit hit the fan. Beatrice and I decided to end our affair. I moved out that day. That Friday I had just got home from work and someone knocked on the door. I opened it before I looked out it was Eddie. He didn't say anything he just started punching me I tried to block some of the blows but they were coming fast and hard. I tripped and I thought he was going to kill me."

"I don't know where Beatrice came from but she got him to stop. He must have loved her a lot because they never broke up. I didn't go to the doctor for my eye. I was too embarrassed to explain why it happened."

"Needless to say our friendship was over.

So I knew I would be staying with my mother for while. Momma told me that Richards never came back to the house.

"She would take Zoey to see him. I wasn't crazy about that arrangement at all but, I was glad I didn't have to look in his face. As time went on I was changing. It got to the point that the only thing that mattered to me was my momma not knowing how I was spending my nights. I was in every strip club in town. I was pulling up to every corner picking up any one that would get in the car. I was like a fat person addicted to cake."

"Sometimes I blamed Richards and Beatrice. Other times I knew it was me. I couldn't feel anything. Finally it all came to a head when I got caught in a raid at one of those houses."

"Of all people my pastor was the one who came and got me out. He suggested I go to therapy and maybe go back to school. It was hard but I wanted to show momma and him that I hadn't completely gone down the drain."

"Things seemed to be getting better. In time school wasn't as hard as I thought it was going to be. Eventually I got all the certificates and diplomas I needed. I could work in any engineering position I wanted. I know Momma was proud. I was making good money.

"I even offered to put momma and Zoey in another house. She just thought that was a waste of money. She was happy to see me going in the right direction."

"I was around twenty five and Zoey was about to graduate. Every now and then Zoey gave us hope that she wouldn't be anything like him. But for the most part she was still a spoiled brat. Richards gave her everything she wanted. But nothing was ever enough for Zoey."

"That's all I can tell you right now. Unless you want to start on the last chapter."

"What do you mean the last chapter?" Cynthia asked.

"The next time we talk I will tell you what really happened to that bastard," Deacon said.

"Although I know it won't be good I can't wait to hear it. Deacon you have poured your heart out these past few months," Cynthia said.

"I can't tell you how much I appreciate you letting me write this story with you. I can tell you that my publisher is really interested in publishing this book."

"You don't know how much you have helped me by being able to finally tell the truth. Before I forget I would be happy to work with your publisher, "Deacon said.

Cynthia put away the recorder and computer. They went down to the lake to see if Delia was ready to go. She was just putting the last fish in the cooler. Deacon carried them back to the car for her. He promised to meet them back to the house to help clean the fish.

Deacon stopped by his house first. When he walked into the living room he looked around. This was the first time he looked around the living room and, it hit him that this was where it all started.

He only let his self think about the time he

spent with his mother in that house. He thought even though the book may have brought back some painful memories she would understand he needed to do that.

CHAPTER TEN

Thou Shall Not

Deacon was looking forward to that fish dinner.
Delia caught a bucket of trout big and small.
Cynthia hated cleaning fish. She said something
about it made her feel like a cave man. Her mom
reminded her she was going to eat them like a
cave man so keep cleaning.

Sissy had been invited to come to dinner. She
was supposed to help clean fish also. Somehow
she managed only to make it just in time for
dinner. Of course they didn't let her live it down.
They had a good time the conversation was like
a family get together. Deacon looked from one
of the girls to the other. At one point he was

laughing at Cynthia so hard he swallowed a small bone.

Between the three of them beating on his back it finally went down. The jester brought tears to his eyes. The girls just thought his eyes were watering from choking. These ladies were becoming like family to him.

After the table was cleared, Deacon and Sissy knew they had to be up early so they prepared to leave.

Everybody gave each other a hug. Cynthia told Deacon she would probably be able to meet with him that weekend.

The week went by fast. As usual the fresh air around the cabin gave Cynthia and Deacon a sense of peace. This time Deacon provided breakfast. He told Cynthia that he didn't know what she did to the coffee but it was the best he ever tasted.

"I can't believe we are almost at the end of the story. I can tell you that your story is going to be very unique. Some authors can't keep your attention from beginning to end. I can't imagine anyone wanting to put this one down," Cynthia said.

"Well young lady are you ready to get started?"

"Sure, but can we talk about your Mom a little bit?"

"Was she still living when that bastard died?"

"No momma died before all that happened. I know his death would not have meant anything to her."

H

"But me going to prison for his murder would have been enough to give her a heart attack."

"I can't tell you how many times she came to me in my dreams. She just kept saying over and over it would all be over soon. I'd wake up in a cold sweat feeling sad. Now I know what she meant.

"I thank God for Miss Justine and Miss Addie. And even though Eddie and Beatrice came to the funeral, it was years before they came to see me in jail. It was kind of weird talking to them about old times."

"I remember almost getting into another fight with the jack-o-lantern and the demon seed. He thought he was going to step up in my momma's funeral like it was okay. My pastor at that time stopped me by saying that my mom would not want that to happen. Zoey made a big scene screaming that I was just being hateful as usual."

"Did Zoey ever find out what he did to you?

"No but, she will now," Deacon said.

"I am glad that you and Eddie and Beatrice were friends again."

"Yeah, to this day I am so grateful that Eddie forgave me.

"I understand you guys used to go to the same church as my mom."

"Yes, then my mother decided she needed a change. So she joined Mount Calvary," Deacon said.

"I remember when our school went on a field trip to Mount Calvary. We went to see the room used for the Underground Railroad. I remember it had a dirt floor. There was a small wooden table and a homemade cot they said the slaves built. What made it so unique no one knew it was there because the entrance was covered with ivy and flowers. All the kids ooooed when they saw the door open," Cynthia said.

"I guess every kid in the neighborhood took that tour. In spite of everything that happened Mount Calvary Baptist Church's reputation was restored. After all it wasn't the building it was the people," Deacon said.

Cynthia gave him a strange look. Deacon sat down in the chair facing Cynthia.

"What I'm going to tell you now are facts that came out once the police found out the truth. Unfortunately Richards also joined Mount Calvary."

"Once the truth was out my lawyer let me see the proof for myself."

"Zoey and Reverend Gray were having an affair. They were caught on tape doing their thing in that room," Deacon said.

"You're kidding, I can't believe it," Cynthia said.

"Trust me there's more, I knew she was a liar and, a very convincing one," Deacon said.

"I don't doubt that at all. But what has that got to do with Richard's death?" Cynthia asked.

"The night Richards was killed I was out of town. I did that lot after momma died. I'd find a rest stop and, sleep and wake up and, drive some more."

"When I saw the beginning of the tape I was very annoyed with my lawyer. I asked him,

"What the hell was I looking at? The last thing I wanted to see was her face or any other part of her.

"He said once I got past the mushy stuff that there would be something that would interest me very much. So I kept watching. Zoey and Gray were standing up against the wall kissing. Then he undid her skirt and was feeling her up. She did the same. The next thing you know she took his pants off. He turns her around and starts doing her from behind."

"After that Zoey falls to her knees and did things with her tongue I had never seen before. Gray realizes they had not closed the door that led to the inside of the church. So he stopped to shut it. Then it became pitch dark."

"Yes I remember some of the kids were

scared, it was so dark in there the teacher took the flash light off the table and turned it on," Cynthia said.

"They kept that flashlight down there for that reason. It's one like a construction worker would use," Deacon said.

"Well I was about to get up and leave when the lawyer told me it wasn't over. You could hear them making all kinds of noises. Then I heard footsteps."

"Once the person got in front of the door his face is on camera. It was Richards and, he's banging on the door and yelling. He's telling whoever is in there to open the door. He said he was going to call the police. That's when you hear Zoey and Gray say no don't do that."

"And that's when Richards gets crazy and

started trying to kick the door down. He's saying he is going to kill Gray. When Zoey opens the door she screams at Richards for ruining her night. She screams in his face that nobody is going to stop her from being first lady. She wanted to know what he was doing there. He says he forgot some papers for a church meeting. Then he slaps her so hard she falls to the floor."

"Gray is still trying to get his pants on. Richards runs up to him and starts choking him. Zoey struggles to her feet and grabs that flashlight off the table and begins hitting Richards over the head. She kept hitting him until he fell."

"She dropped the flashlight and grabbed Gray and starts crying. She said she had to do it or Richards would have killed him. He calms her down and says that he is going to take care of it. They decide to take the money and cards out of Richard's wallet.

"Then Zoey said she'd put the empty wallet in Richard's car and drive it out of town. She would stay on the back roads. When she got where she was going she would call Gray so he could pick her up."

"Gray said he would take care of the body. So he decides to dig up that dirt floor and bury Richard's body in that room."

"In spite of all their plotting and scheming they forgot the cameras were on that night."

"If they had a tape of that night why did they arrest you?" Cynthia asked.

"Oh the plot thickens," Deacon said.

"Nobody knew where the tape was but

Mr. Simmons. He was in charge of the sound system, the cameras and, mikes."

"He didn't check the tape until that following week. That's when he decided to blackmail Gray and Zoey. When I come home from my drive Zoey tells me Richards is missing. She said the police want to talk to me."

"I go down to the station thinking no problem. I didn't have anything to do with it. As it turns out Zoey was wearing my hoodie that night and Richard's blood was all over it. She was wearing gloves when she took it off and left it in Richard's car. Somehow not even a hair of hers was in the car. Unfortunately I couldn't prove where I had been the day before."

"The next part of the story I like to call poetic justice. Eddie and Beatrice told me about it. They said Gray was preaching up a storm one Sunday. The ladies were shouting and falling out. The ushers were running from person to person fanning like crazy."

"The next thing you know three big ass rats came running up the steps. One shot across the pulpit and the other two terrorized the people in the pews. Some were stomping the floor. Others were standing on the seats," Deacon said with a smile.

"That's when Gray must have remembered that he forgot to move the body. He starts clenching his chest and had a heart attack and died right there. You would think that would have made Zoey confess, not a chance."

"A month later Mr. Simmons has a bad

car accident in the new car he bought with his blackmail money."

"He decides to give a death bed confession and, tells police where the key to the box of tapes are hidden. They arrested Zoey that night. My lawyer contacted me the next day. They showed the tapes to the D.A. and started the paper work so I could be free."

"Have you talked with her since then?" Cynthia asked.

"No, why?"

"I thought she might have the decency to apologize."

"You would think so but Hell will freeze over before she would apologize."

"They say she went in kicking and screaming.

The funny thing is I don't hate her. I just can't stand to see her face right now."

"I'm surprised she didn't have a fit about you living in the house," Cynthia said.

"She didn't really have any choice in that matter. Half of the house belonged to my mother and half belonged to him. That was never changed. I knew she was not coming back any time soon."

"I'll do what I can to keep it but I don't plan on living there forever. I want to take some of that award money and buy my own house. Then I'll rent that one maybe the new family will be able to enjoy it."

"Well I can't wait to see what my publisher has to say about the story. They are worried that

Zoey would not let you put her part of the story in the book.

"I'd hate to have to wait until Hell freezes over to get her consent," Cynthia said.

"We also need to get Reverend Gray's wife to let us put him in the book. I'm guessing she'll be the easiest to talk too. Anyone else that is still living we'll change their names."

"I never knew telling the truth could be so complicated," Deacon said.

"The first thing I need to do is edit the story. Then we'll see if we can get around getting Zoey's permission. Like we said I don't think the first lady will be a problem. I know you want to tell the whole truth but you might want to consider not talking about your affair with

Beatrice. No need in rubbing salt into that old wound."

"That's true I guess we can omit that part. I just needed to come clean about everything," Deacon said.

"Also when you have time to think about it let me know what kind of cover you want," Cynthia said.

"Wow I had not even thought about that. If you have any ideas I'd be glad to listen," Deacon said.

"If you don't mind let's get out of here and get something to eat."

"That sounds like a plan. Cynthia I can't thank you enough. You will never know what you did for me by helping tell my story. Not only that you and your mother made me feel like family. Please tell her how much I appreciated that. I didn't know how people were going to treat me when I got out. There is always somebody that never believes you're innocent."

"I catch people looking at me funny when I'm in the store. Maybe this book will free me once and for all."

Cynthia assured Deacon that she was more than happy to help him. She hugged him and he held her for a minute or two. She looked up at him and smiled.

"Guess we'd better go," she said.

"Yes, but it's my treat," Deacon said.

"Oh, in that case I think I'll have a steak and some baked chicken on the side. Some greens, potato salad, corn bread, a slice of pie and, maybe a little piece of chocolate cake to take home."

Deacon laughed and took Cynthia by the arm and they headed to the restaurant.

He Shall Strengthen Thine Heart

Deacon stood in the doorway of the kitchen watching his new family. He never thought in a million years that he could ever be this happy. The book had not been published yet. It took Cynthia two years to persuade Deacon to talk to Zoey. She didn't want Zoey's part in the book to be a problem.

Deacon would do anything for Cynthia but, this was the hardest thing she asked him to do. Finally he decided he would go. To his surprised this was not the Zoey he used to know. She had changed a lot, they actually talked. She even apologized for framing him. He accepted her apology and told her about the book. By some miracle she even gave her permission to put her in the book. After a few more visits Deacon told her what really happened with him and Richards. She didn't want to believe it. But she knew Deacon didn't lie.

There were times him and Cynthia would visit her together. He supported her financially. He remembered how hopeless he felt when he was in prison.

Cynthia all his night mares disappeared. Deep down Deacon knew they would never haunt him again.

The End

I wrote this story to give a child hood friend a voice. We grew up at a time when people thought that what parents did to their children was their business. Even as a child I knew that was wrong. I witnessed him being hit and that image stayed with me until now. I always wonder how he is doing. Unfortunately that family moved away before we grew up.

Thank you for reading this story. I hope to inform and uplift and maybe even make readers smile. I'm late on the writing scene but it's a dream I'm so happy to see come true.

Here are a few organizations that I found online that may be helpful to boys and girls that need help:

SCAN (Stop Child Abuse Now)

Richmond, Va. 804-257-7226

National Child Abuse Hotline

1-800-422-4453

UMFS

1866-252-7772

Please don't be afraid to talk to your school counselor or a teacher.

The Boys and Girls Club in your area may be able to help.

Check with the YMCA

You may also want to contact Social services in your town.

Printed in the United States
By Bookmasters